People Have Their Say

Nicolas Brasch

Australia • Brazil • Japan • Korea • Mexico • Singapore • Spain • United Kingdom • United States

People Have Their Say

Fast Forward
Silver Level 23

Text: Nicolas Brasch
Editor: Cameron Macintosh
Design: Stella Vassiliou
Series design: James Lowe
Production controller: Seona Galbally
Photo research: Fiona Smith
Audio recordings: Juliet Hill, Picture Start
Spoken by: Matthew King and Abbe Holmes
Reprint: Jennifer Foo

Acknowledgements
The author and publisher would like to acknowledge permission to reproduce material from the following sources: Photographs byAAP Image, p 13/ Mick Tsikas, p 22; AFP/Getty Images/RAFA RIVAS, p 15; Alamy/Dennis MacDonald, p 11/ Richard Levine, p 11 top left; Fotolia, pp 3, 20; Mary Evans Picture Library, pp 6, 7, 9; Newsphotos, cover top, p 1 bottom, 4, 12, 18/ NewsPix/Bell Shane, p 17/ Bob Fenney, p 23/ Cumberland@MartinLange, p 10/ Jeff Herbert, cover bottom, pp 1 top, 5, 16/ John Grainger, p 14/ Ross Schultz, back cover, p 19; Photolibrary/The Print Collector, p 8.

ISBN 978 0 17 012700 4
ISBN 978 0 17 012693 9 (set)

Cengage Learning Australia
Level 7, 80 Dorcas Street
South Melbourne, Victoria Australia 3205
Phone: 1300 790 853

Cengage Learning New Zealand
Unit 4B Rosedale Office Park
331 Rosedale Road, Albany, North Shore NZ 0632
Phone: 0508 635 766

For learning solutions, visit cengage.com.au

Printed in Australia by Ligare Pty Ltd
6 7 8 9 10 11 12 21 20 19 18 17

THE UNIVERSITY OF MELBOURNE

Evaluated in independent research by staff from the Department of Language, Literacy and Arts Education at the University of Melbourne.

People Have Their Say

Nicolas Brasch

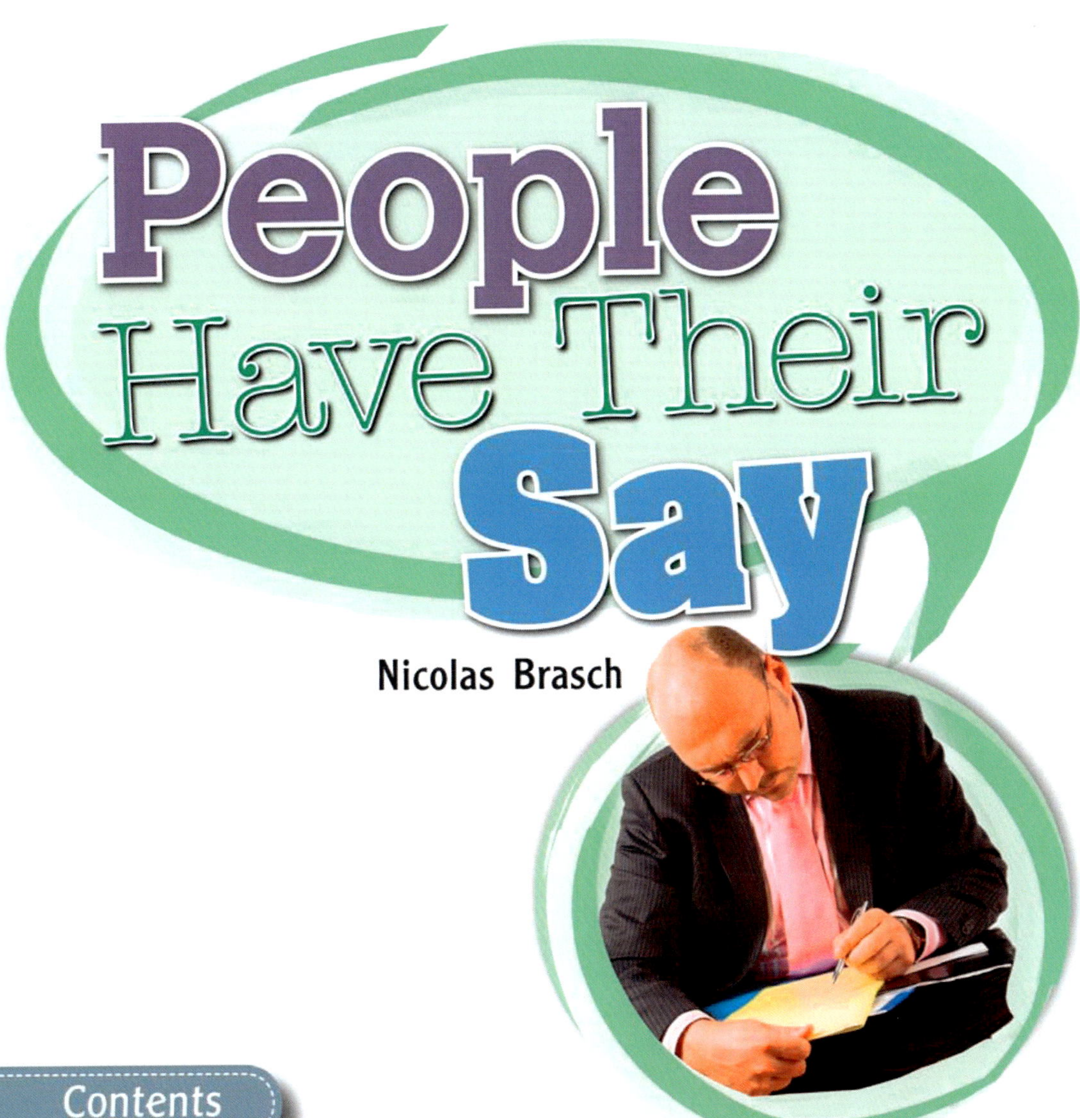

Contents

Chapter 1

INTRODUCTION

There are many ways in which people have their say about how they are **governed**.
These range from common activities that most people do, like voting, to less common activities, like joining a **political party**.

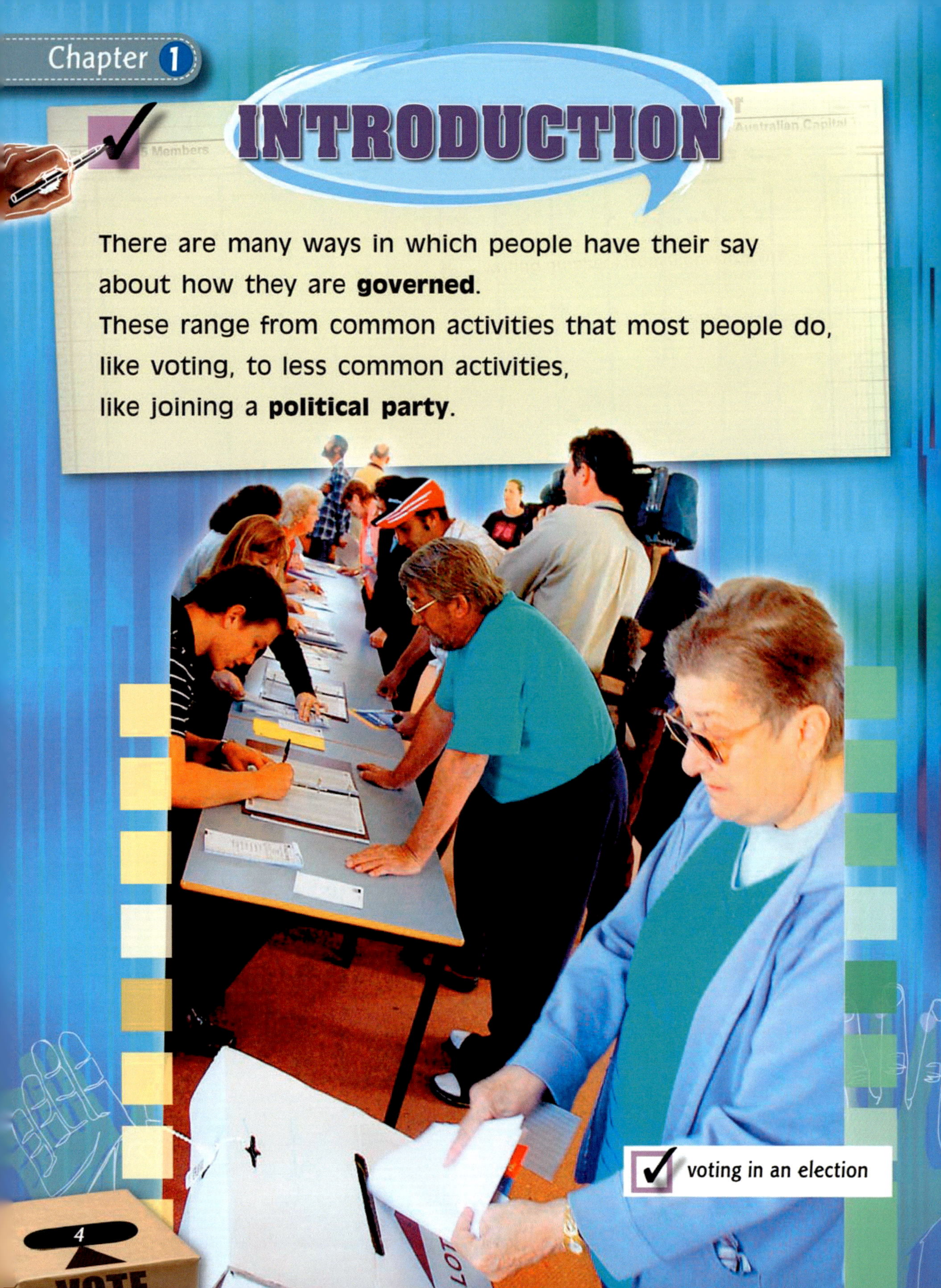

voting in an election

voting at a public meeting

Whichever way people choose to express their views, each way has the same purpose – to enable members of the community to participate in the democratic process.

Chapter 2

A SHORT HISTORY OF DEMOCRACY

Democracy is a system of government. It involves members of the community having a say in the way they are governed. The ancient Greeks are believed to be the first people to form a democratic society, about 2600 years ago.

The word 'democracy' comes from the Greek words 'demos', which means 'the people', and 'kratein', which means 'to rule'. So, democracy means 'rule by the people'.

Ancient Greek Empire, around 550 BC

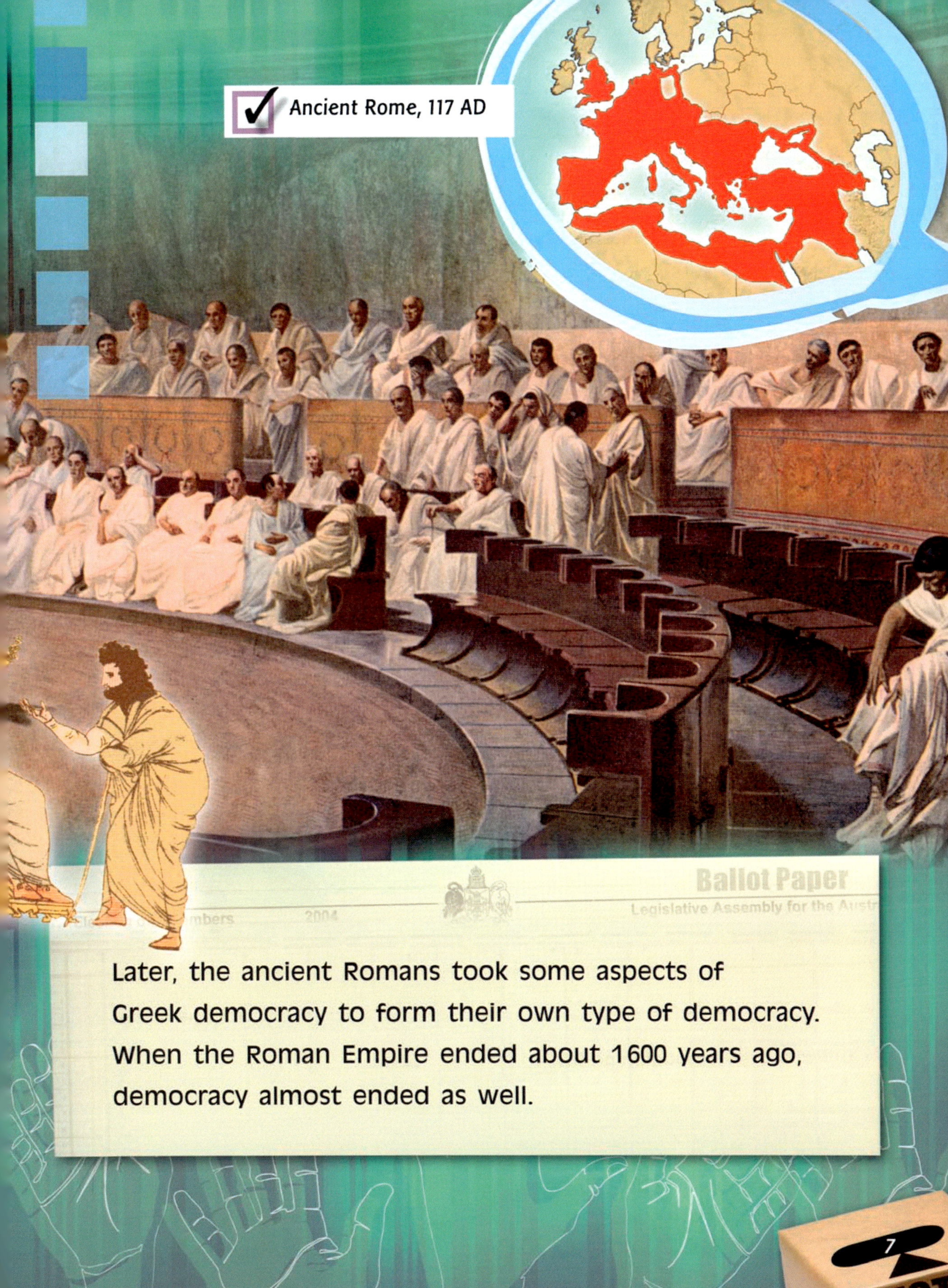

Later, the ancient Romans took some aspects of Greek democracy to form their own type of democracy. When the Roman Empire ended about 1600 years ago, democracy almost ended as well.

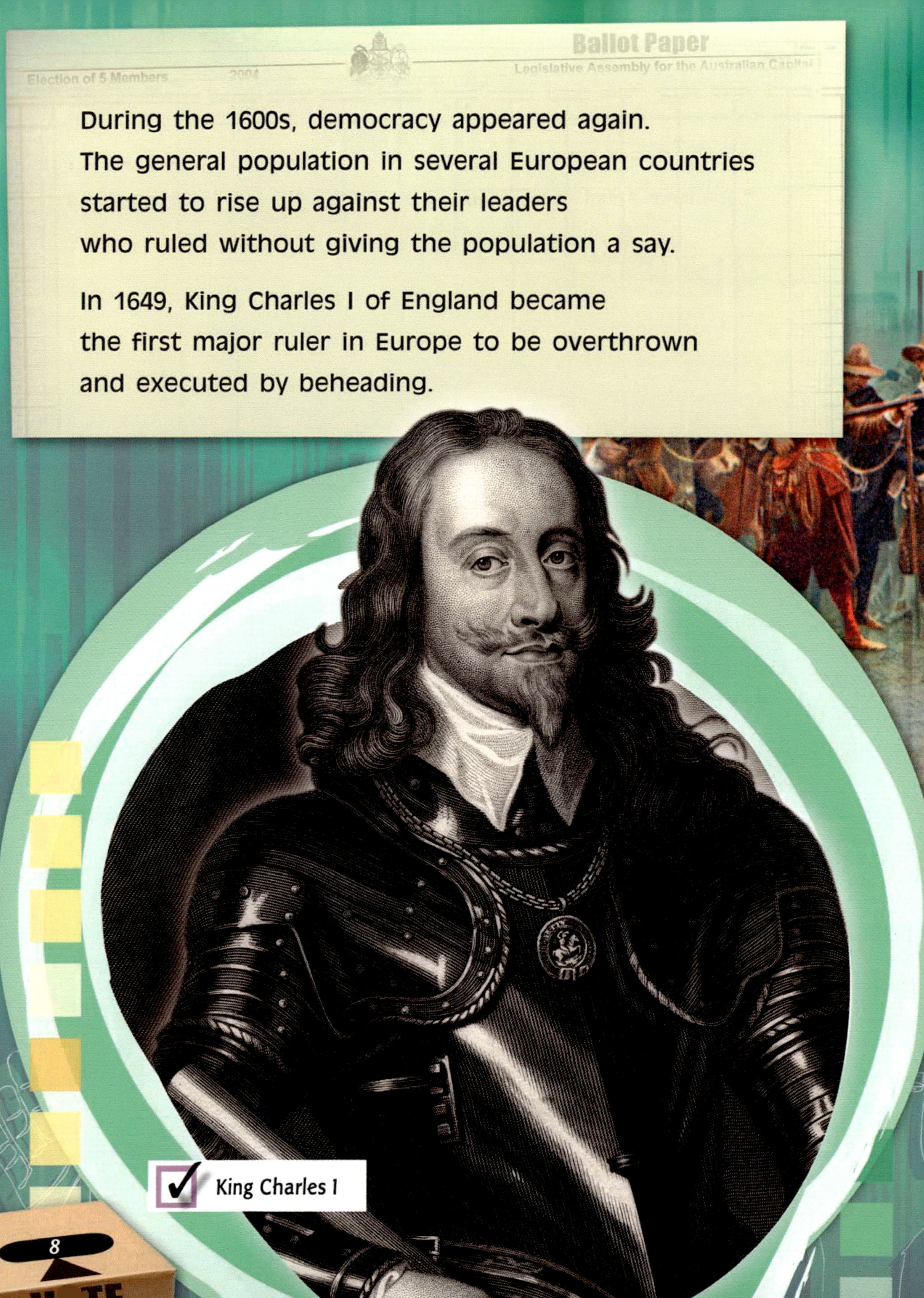

During the 1600s, democracy appeared again. The general population in several European countries started to rise up against their leaders who ruled without giving the population a say.

In 1649, King Charles I of England became the first major ruler in Europe to be overthrown and executed by beheading.

King Charles I

King Charles I, being led to his execution

The execution of King Charles I led to the formation of an English government based on democratic ideas. Other European countries followed, including France. Then, democracy gradually spread throughout much of Europe and further around the world.

Running Words 218

Chapter 3

VOTING

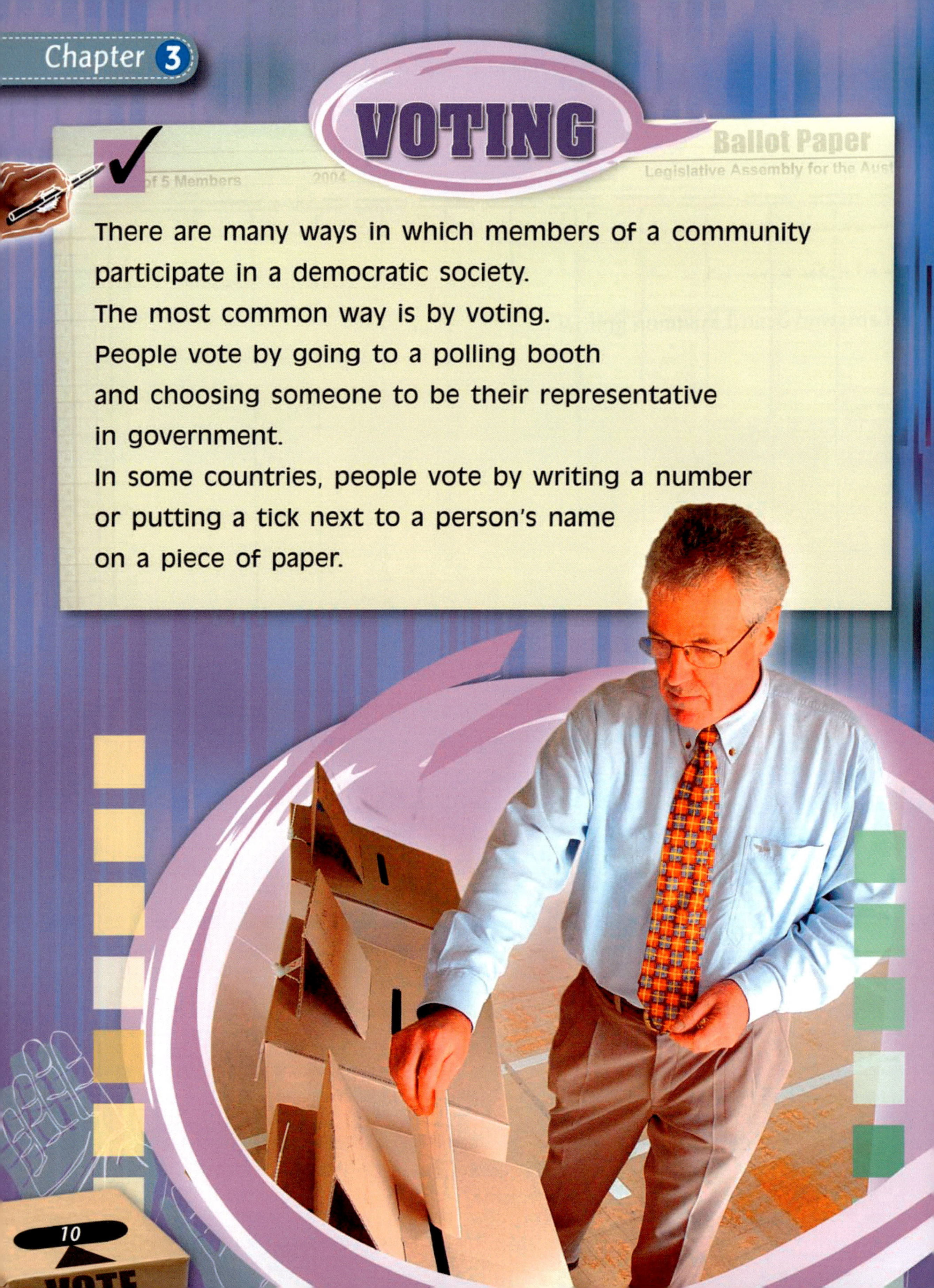

There are many ways in which members of a community participate in a democratic society.
The most common way is by voting.
People vote by going to a polling booth and choosing someone to be their representative in government.
In some countries, people vote by writing a number or putting a tick next to a person's name on a piece of paper.

In other countries, people vote by pulling a lever to indicate which **candidate** they prefer.

In still other countries, people vote using a small machine that punches a hole in a piece of cardboard next to the name of a candidate.

18 or 21?

In some democratic countries, people are eligible to vote at age 18. In other democratic countries, people are eligible to vote at age 21. People younger than 18 are not considered to be mature enough to help decide who should run the government of a country.

Compulsory or Voluntary?

In some democratic countries, like Australia, voting is compulsory.

This means that people who are eligible to vote must do so, otherwise they will be fined.

In other democratic countries, like the United States, voting is voluntary.

This means that people who are eligible to vote can decide whether or not they want to vote in a particular election.

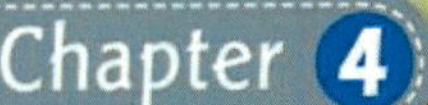

JOINING A POLITICAL PARTY

Voting may be the most common way people have a say in the way they are governed, but it isn't the only way. People who have an interest in government and politics have the opportunity to join a political party. This enables them to have a say in the **policies** that their preferred political party takes to an election.

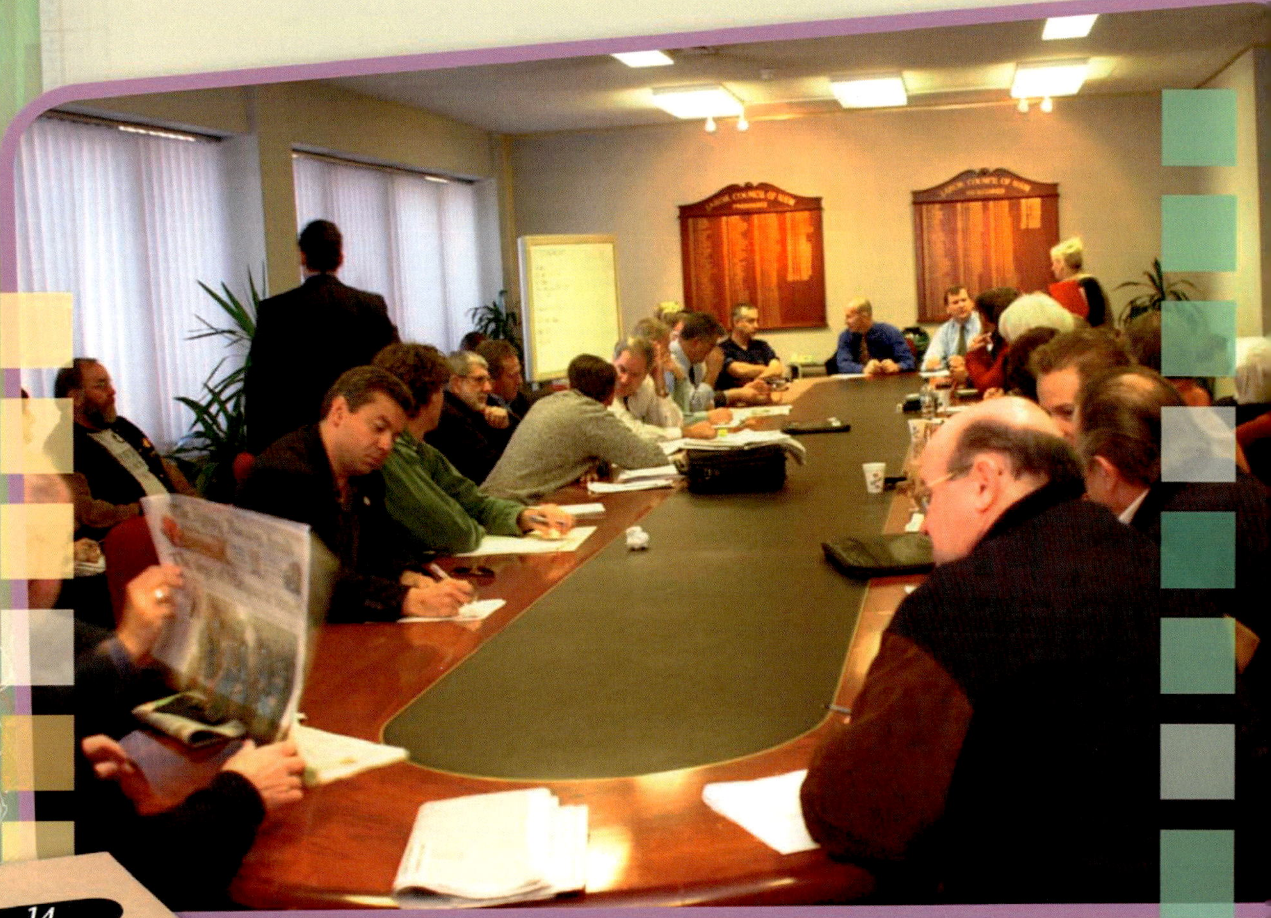

For example, if a person disagrees with his or her preferred party's view on a particular issue, like immigration or taxation, he or she can speak up at meetings and try to get other members of the party to help change the policy. A political party should follow the policies that the majority of its members want.

Choosing a Candidate

Members of political parties are responsible for choosing the people who will try to represent the party in parliament.

The members choose their candidate and then help to **campaign** for that candidate at an election.

In the lead-up to an election, this help includes:

- putting leaflets into letterboxes
- putting up posters in their neighbourhood
- handing out leaflets at the polling booth
- scrutineering.

Scrutineering

Scrutineering involves overseeing the counting of ballot papers when the voting has finished. It also involves making sure that officials counting the ballot papers don't make a mistake that costs the scrutineer's preferred candidate any votes.

Chapter 5

PUBLIC MEETINGS AND PROTESTS

Some people want to get involved in certain political issues rather than with a political party.
These people can go to public meetings or public protests.

A public meeting involves the discussion of a particular issue.
For example, the people from a rural community might discuss whether or not to build wind turbines in the area.

Ballot Paper

Election of 5 Members 2004

Legislative Assembly for the Australian Capital

A public protest involves a march through the streets, or a public gathering where people show their opposition or support for a certain issue or policy.

During the 1960s and 1970s, huge public protests against the Vietnam War helped bring the war to an end.

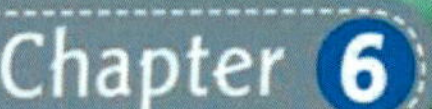

LETTER WRITING

Some people have their say about issues by writing letters. They may write letters to their local councillor or member of parliament to put across their point of view.

They might write a letter to a newspaper in the hope that it is published and their view gets read by many people.

LETTERS TO THE EDITOR

To the Editor,

I cannot believe that the government is thinking of expanding the Springfield Airport. Residents who live near the airport already put up with a great deal of noise. An expansion of the airport will increase the number of planes and therefore the amount of noise.

A more logical solution would be to build an airport about the same size as Springfield Airport in Port Vale. That way, the noise and air pollution would be spread and the people of Port Vale would not have to travel to Springfield to catch a plane.

Yours sincerely,

Bill O'Brien,
Springfield

Dear Editor

I am very
exercise sp
there is no
and to enj
There are
Reserve w
leash' area
would be
hygiene of
provide su

Yours sinc

Alice Nguy
East Sprin

TALKBACK RADIO

Talkback radio gives everybody a chance to have their say. It allows members of the public to ring a radio station and present their view on air.